Soap Bubble Magic

SOAP BUBBLE MAGIC

By Seymour Simon

Illustrated by Stella Ormai

Lothrop,
Lee & Shepard Books
New York

LIBRARY OF CONGRESS CATALOGING IN PUBLICATION DATA
Simon, Seymour.
Soap bubble magic.
Summary: Explains what soap bubbles are, how they are formed, and what can be
done with them.
1. Soap-bubbles—Juvenile literature. [1. Bubbles. 2. Water. 3. Amusements.]
I. Ormai, Stella, ill.   II. Title.
QC183.S475   1985   793.5   84-4432
ISBN 0-688-02684-2
ISBN 0-688-02685-0 (lib. bdg.)

Have you ever watched soap bubbles?

They float so lightly in the air.
Some burst quickly. Poof!
In an instant, they are gone.

Some soap bubbles last longer.
They bob up and down in the air.

Some are double bubbles.
They are big and slow moving.

What happens when you try to catch them?
Double poof!

Let's make soap bubbles,
and find out about them.
Here's how:
Spread newspapers on a table
so you won't get the table wet.
Put four tablespoons of a liquid
dishwashing detergent
in a glass half full of clean water.
Then stir.

Make a loop at one end
of a piece of stiff wire.

Dip the loop into the soapy water.
Slowly wave the loop through the air.
What happens?

Quickly wave the loop through the air.
What happens now?

Does moving fast make more bubbles
than moving slowly?
Which way makes bigger bubbles?

Try blowing through the loop.
Blow hard.
Then blow softly.
Which way makes bigger bubbles?

Now you know that slow-moving air
passing through the loop
makes a few big bubbles.
Fast-moving air makes lots of small bubbles.
Does it matter whether you blow through the loop
or move the loop through the air?

Try it again and watch.
Now say what you think.

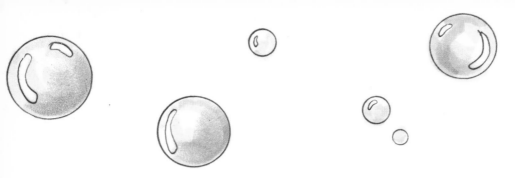

You can see soap bubbles in the air,
but can you see the air in soap bubbles?
Catch a soap bubble with your dry hands.
When the bubble breaks,
what is left on your hands?
Just a tiny bit of water.
How could such a tiny bit of water
make such a big bubble?
The answer is that air
was in the bubble.
Soap bubbles are also air bubbles.
When you blow a soap bubble,
you put air inside a soap-and-water skin.

Water has a skin where it meets the air.

Try this:

Fill a glass to the very top with water.

Now use a small dropper to add more water.

Add one drop at a time.

Soon the surface of the water will bulge

above the top of the glass.

Why doesn't the water spill over?

Because it is held there by the water skin at the top.

You can even float a needle on a water skin.

Here's how:

Put water in a wide glass bowl.

Carefully lay a needle
flat on top of the water.

Look through the glass from the side.

See that the water skin dips down
under the weight of the needle.

The water skin is holding up the needle.

NEEDLE

What happens if you drop a needle
point first into a water skin?

Try it and see.

Now you know the "magic" that lets
some insects such as water striders
skate on the top of a pond
without breaking through.
The water skin holds up the insects,
and they don't get wet.

Of course, you can break through a water skin.

A water skin pulls together so strongly
that a water bubble will break when
it reaches the surface.
Here's how you can see that this is true:
Put a straw into a glass of water.
Blow bubbles in the water.
What happens to the bubbles?

All the bubbles break when they reach the top.
The water skin pulls together
and breaks the bubbles.

Now mix some soap or detergent with water in a glass.
Blow bubbles with the straw.
(Be careful not to swallow the water.)
What happens to the bubbles this time?
The soap weakens the pull of the water skin.
The soap bubbles can last longer in the air than the plain water bubbles can.

Here's another way to see
how soap weakens the water skin.
Fill a dish with water.
Shake pepper grains all over the water.
Wait until they stop moving around.
Now take a small piece of wet soap
and dip it into the water
on one side of the dish.

Like magic, the pepper grains start to move.
Do you know why?
It's because the clear water on one side
pulls the pepper grains strongly.
The soapy water on the other side
does not pull so strongly.
So the pepper grains move
toward the clear water.

Here's how to make a boat
that moves like soapy magic.
Make a little boat
out of a piece of aluminum foil.
Rub some wet soap or some liquid detergent
on the back of the boat.
Float the boat in a bathtub
or a large bowl of water.
Away it goes!
The boat moves from soapy water
to clear water.
Now you know why.
Clear water has a stronger pull
than soapy water.

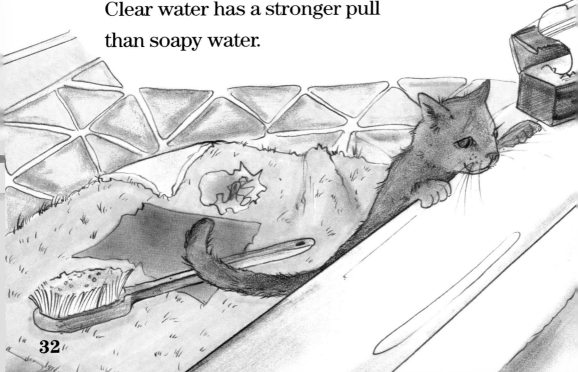

Do soap bubbles always look round
like a ball?
Watch them as you blow.
When you make soap bubbles,
they are different shapes.
Some are long and thin.

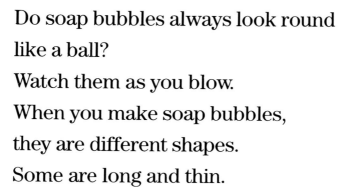

Some are fat at one end like a pear.
What shapes can you see?
What happens when the different shaped
bubbles float free in the air?

Like magic, all the single bubbles become round.

Look at the bubbles that stay together.

Where they stick to each other,

these bubbles are flat.

Can you catch soap bubbles in the air?
Catch them on a piece of paper.
Catch them with your hand.
Each time you catch one, what happens?
Is there any way to catch a soap bubble
without breaking it?
Let's try.

Catch a soap bubble with a soapy loop.
Catch a soap bubble with soapy hands.
Do you know what "magic" lets you
catch soap bubbles without breaking them?
Try again to see if you are right.
Ask a friend to try.

DRY HANDS

SOAPY
LOOP

SOAPY
HANDS

Can you make a bubble stay up longer
in the air by blowing on it?
Blow down on a bubble.
Blow up on a bubble.
Air keeps bubbles up.
Air can also push bubbles down.

It depends upon which way air is moving.
When you blow up, bubbles will stay up longer.
When you blow down, bubbles go down faster.
Moving air is called wind.
What do you think happens when you
blow bubbles outdoors on a windy day?
Up, up, and away!

You can see through the air around you.
You can see through the air
in soap bubbles too.
Catch a soap bubble with a soapy loop.
Don't break it.
Look through a soap bubble at a friend.
How does your friend look?
Look through a soap bubble
at your dog or cat.
How does your pet look?
The curved water skin of a bubble
bends the light rays going through it.
That's why your friend and your pet
look so funny through a soap bubble.

43

Soap bubbles look shiny.
You can see many colors and lights
in the soapy water of a bubble.

A soap bubble is also like a mirror.
You can see yourself in a soap bubble.
You can see the room behind you.
You can see your friends making bubbles.
What else do you see
when you look at a soap bubble?

Play with soap bubbles
and think about them.
Look at things that interest you.
Try new things.

Think about what you see and do.
The "magic" of soap bubbles is that
they show us things about the world around us.

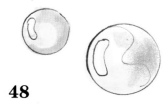